O9-BUB-402

A science

The Magic School Bus®
CHAPTER BOOK

The Wild
WHALE WATCH

SCHOLASTIC INC.
New York   Toronto   London   Auckland   Sydney
Mexico City   New Delhi   Hong Kong   Buenos Aires

Written by Eva Moore.

Illustrations by John Speirs.

Based on *The Magic School Bus* books
written by Joanna Cole and illustrated by Bruce Degen.

The author would like to acknowledge Caroline M. DeLong
of the Marine Mammal Research Program at the Hawaii Institute
of Marine Biology for her advice in preparing this manuscript.

If you purchased this book without a cover, you should be aware that this book is stolen property. It was reported as "unsold and destroyed" to the publisher, and neither the author nor the publisher has received any payment for this "stripped book."

No part of this publication may be reproduced in whole or in part, or stored in a retrieval system, or transmitted in any form or by any means, electronic, mechanical, photocopying, recording, or otherwise, without written permission of the publisher. For information regarding permission, write to Scholastic Inc., Attention: Permissions Department, 557 Broadway, New York, NY 10012.

ISBN 0-439-10990-6

Copyright © 2000 by Joanna Cole and Bruce Degen. Published by Scholastic Inc. All rights reserved. SCHOLASTIC, THE MAGIC SCHOOL BUS, and associated logos are trademarks and/or registered trademarks of Scholastic Inc.

60 59 58 57 56 55 54 53   12 13 14 15 16/0

Printed in the U.S.A.   40

INTRODUCTION

My name is Wanda. I am one of the kids in Ms. Frizzle's class.

Maybe you have heard of Ms. Frizzle. (Sometimes we just call her the Friz.) She is a terrific teacher — but a little strange. The Friz *loves* science, and she knows *everything*.

She takes us on lots of field trips in the Magic School Bus. Believe me, it's not called *magic* for nothing! We never know what's going to happen when we get on that bus.

Ms. Frizzle likes to surprise us, but we can usually tell when she is planning a special lesson — we just look at what she's wearing.

One day she came into class wearing a yellow dress covered with purple blobs. Up close, we could tell that the blobs were really little whale shapes. I had seen whales on TV, but I never thought I'd get to see one in person. Thanks to Ms. Frizzle, I got closer to a whale than I'd ever dreamed. I'll tell you what happened. . . .

CHAPTER 1

"Ms. Frizzle is late," Tim said. He looked up at the clock on the classroom wall. "She's usually here before we get in."

We were all sitting at our desks, ready to begin the first lesson of the day — science.

"Yeah," D.A. said, "and she's hardly ever late for science."

Just then the door opened. Ms. Frizzle came waltzing in, carrying a large, lumpy envelope.

"Good morning, class!" she sang out. "I'm sorry to keep you waiting. I had to stop by the office to pick up some important mail." She held up the envelope.

"Here are the tickets for our next field trip," she announced. "And I promise you're all going to have a whale of a good time."

"I get it!" Keesha said. "I bet we're going on a whale watch!"

"Right you are, Keesha," Ms. Frizzle said. "I asked my old friend Captain Gil to send me tickets for the whale-watch cruise on his boat, the *Neptune*. We're going today."

"Yay!" Ralphie yelled. "I can hardly wait! I've always wanted to see a real live whale."

"Me too," Tim said. "I hope we get to see a blue whale. They are huge!"

"We might see a blue whale," Ms. Frizzle said. "I can't promise. Different kinds of whales live all over the world. Today we're going to see whales that live off the New England coast."

Ms. Frizzle pulled a bunch of booklets from the envelope and handed them out.

"Captain Gil knows a lot about whales. Here's a copy of his handbook for each of you. It's full of fabulous whale facts. They're amazing mammals."

Big Blue
by Tim

The blue whale is the largest animal that has ever lived on Earth — it's longer than six elephants and weighs more than a seismosaurus, one of the most gigantic dinosaurs ever known.

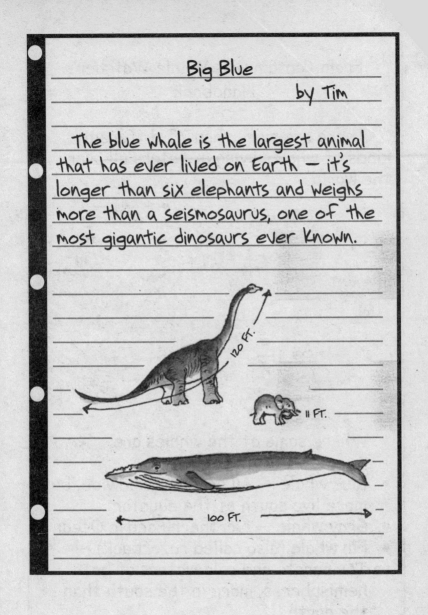

120 FT.

11 FT.

100 FT.

From Captain Gil's Whale Watcher's Handbook

There are more than 75 different kinds of whales living in waters all over the world.

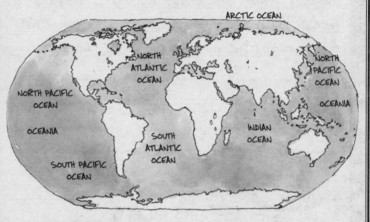

Where some of the whales are:

- **Blue whale** — All oceans worldwide, but more live south of the equator
- **Gray whale** — Northern Pacific Ocean
- **Fin whale** (also called razorback) — Temperate and cold waters of both hemispheres, more in the south than the north

- **Minke whale** — Tropical, temperate, and polar waters of both hemispheres
- **Humpback whale** — Worldwide
- **Right whale** — Temperate and cold waters of the northern Pacific and Atlantic Oceans, and of the southern Pacific, Atlantic, and Indian Oceans
- **Bowhead whale** — Arctic Ocean and cold waters of the northern Atlantic and Pacific Oceans
- **Orca** (also called killer whale) — Worldwide
- **Pilot whale** — Northern Atlantic Ocean and Mediterranean Sea; also southern Atlantic, Indian, and Pacific Oceans
- **Sperm whale** — Worldwide
- **Narwhal** — Arctic Ocean, especially around Canada
- **Beluga whale** — Coastal seas of Arctic Ocean; also, Hudson Bay, Gulf of Saint Lawrence, Barents Sea, Gulf of Alaska. Sometimes North Sea and northern Atlantic Ocean

"Wow," Carlos said as he flipped through the handbook, "I never knew there were so many kinds of whales."

"That's right, Carlos," the Friz replied, "and all the whales are divided into two types."

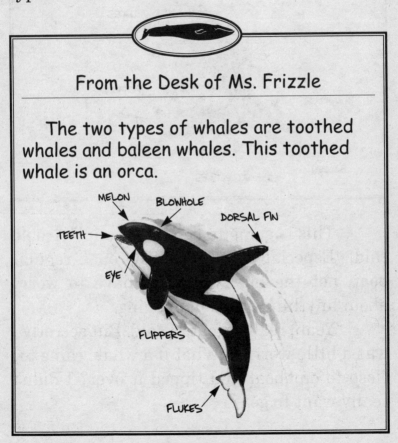

From the Desk of Ms. Frizzle

The two types of whales are toothed whales and baleen whales. This toothed whale is an orca.

MELON

BLOWHOLE

DORSAL FIN

TEETH

EYE

FLIPPERS

FLUKES

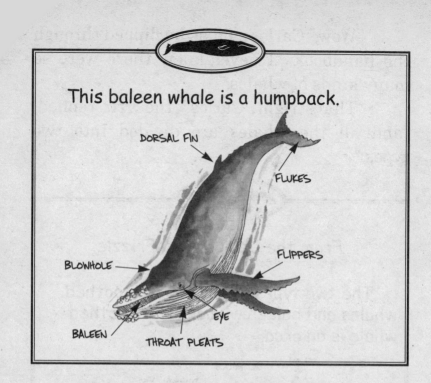

This baleen whale is a humpback.

DORSAL FIN

FLUKES

FLIPPERS

BLOWHOLE

EYE

BALEEN

THROAT PLEATS

"This is going to be a great trip!" Arnold said. "Especially since we'll be on a regular boat, not the bus. We won't have to worry about anything weird happening."

"Yeah, really great," I said. But secretly I was a little worried. What if a whale came too close to our boat and tipped it over? I didn't really want to go.

"What's the big deal about whales, Ms. Frizzle?" I asked. "They're just big fish."

"Oh, no, Wanda. A whale is not a fish at all — it's a mammal," the Friz replied. "You'll have to get your feet wet to understand the wonderful world of whales. To the bus!"

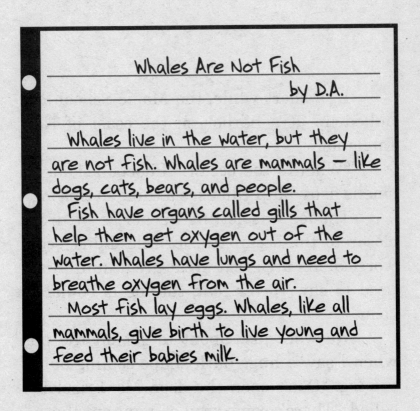

Whales Are Not Fish
by D.A.

Whales live in the water, but they are not fish. Whales are mammals — like dogs, cats, bears, and people.

Fish have organs called gills that help them get oxygen out of the water. Whales have lungs and need to breathe oxygen from the air.

Most fish lay eggs. Whales, like all mammals, give birth to live young and feed their babies milk.

CHAPTER 2

In a short while, the Magic School Bus pulled up at a harbor on the coast of New England.

"Where's the ocean?" Phoebe asked. "It smells fishy, but I can't see a thing in this fog."

The fog was getting thicker as we drove closer to the ocean. Ms. Frizzle didn't seem worried. "As my great-great-great-aunt Misty used to say, 'Never fear, the fog is bound to clear.'"

We were just about to get off the bus when I saw a huge dark shape coming out of the fog. "Don't open the door, Ms. Frizzle!" I called. "There's some kind of giant out there."

"Just a giant at heart," the Friz said as she pulled the lever to open the doors. The "giant" stepped right up the stairs onto the bus. It wasn't a giant after all — just a very large man dressed in a dark blue jacket. He had a bushy white beard and wore a cap with an anchor on it.

"Captain Gil at your service," the man said in a low, rumbling voice. He gave us a little salute and turned to Ms. Frizzle. "I tried to call you, ma'am, but I was too late. I'm afraid I have bad news for the little mateys."

11

The big man looked as if he were about to burst into tears.

"Now, now," the Friz said, "just tell me what happened. Things may not be as bad as you think."

"It's my boat, ma'am," Captain Gil said. "There was a sudden storm last night. The *Neptune* got a bit smashed up. Luckily, the damage can be fixed, but she's not going anywhere today."

"You mean we can't go on the whale watch?" I said, relieved. Everyone else on the bus seemed upset. Then Ms. Frizzle got that twinkle in her eye.

"Didn't I say things may not be as bad as they seem?" She started the engine and the bus moved slowly along the dock. As we picked up speed, wisps of fog crept inside and swirled around us so we couldn't see anything inside or out.

"What's going on?" the captain cried. "Watch out, you're going to drive straight off the dock!"

"We never drove straight into the ocean

at my old school," Phoebe said, her hands covering her eyes.

Suddenly, the fog broke up and there was water all around us. We were in the middle of the ocean — the bus had turned into a boat!

Captain Gil rubbed his eyes. "I must be dreaming," he said.

"No, you're just on the Magic School Bus — er, Boat," Arnold told him with a sigh. "This kind of thing happens all the time."

The captain looked around at the roomy cabin and the shiny instrument panel. "She's a beauty, ma'am," he exclaimed.

"May I take the helm, Ms. Frizzle? I'll keep an eye out for whales and steer us right to them," Captain Gil asked.

"Be my guest!" Ms. Frizzle said. Captain Gil took the wheel, and Liz hopped off Ms. Frizzle's shoulder right onto Captain Gil's. "Splendid," said the captain. "Liz can be my first mate."

Suddenly, a dark shadow caught my eye. It was moving quickly underneath the boat.

Before I could make a sound, it popped out of the water, right next to us. Then another leaped up beside it. "Captain Gil," I screamed. "Help!"

Captain Gil and Ms. Frizzle turned their heads to see. Then a huge smile crossed the captain's face.

"No need to worry, Wanda," he said. "This is welcome company. They are common dolphins." One by one, the black, gray, and cream-colored dolphins dived in and out of the water right next to us.

The dolphins were in front of the boat now, still diving and leaping in graceful curves.

"The dolphins are bow-riding," Captain Gil told us. "The phrase comes from the word we sailors use for the front of the boat — the bow."

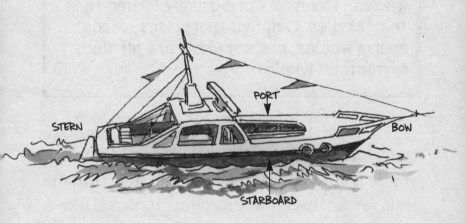

"It says here that dolphins are members of the whale family," said Dorothy Ann, checking her book. "They're called toothed whales."

"It's always a treat to have dolphins swim with us," Captain Gil said.

From Captain Gil's Whale Watcher's Handbook

Toothed Whales

Whales with teeth are called **toothed whales**. The males are usually larger than the females. Dolphins, porpoises, orcas, sperm whales, and narwhals are all kinds of toothed whales.

The dolphins swam on ahead, and we lost sight of them. Captain Gil said, "When you're trying to spot a whale, the first thing to look for is the blow, or spout. It looks like a spurt of mist coming up from the ocean. Whales make blows when they come up to the surface to breathe. Sometimes we can tell what kind of whale is out there just from the blow."

Just then, binoculars dropped down from above our seats.

From Captain Gil's Whale Watcher's Handbook

Whales breathe through blowholes at the top of the head. Because the blowholes are on top, the whale can breathe while most of its body is underwater.

The spray you see is the mist that comes out when the whale exhales. Different kinds of whales have blows of different shapes and sizes. Toothed whales have one blowhole. Baleen whales have two.

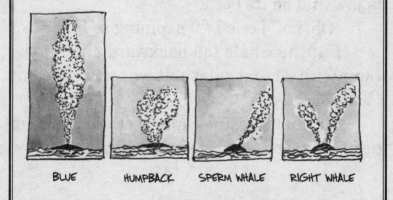

BLUE   HUMPBACK   SPERM WHALE   RIGHT WHALE

Suddenly, Captain Gil cried, "There she blows! Off to port."

We all grabbed our binoculars and looked out to the left. (On a boat, port means left; starboard means right. See the diagram on page 15.)

We could see sprays of water going up all over. Tim checked the spout section in Captain Gil's handbook.

"I think those spouts are from fin whales," he said.

Just then, a huge dark gray whale rose out of the water. It came almost straight up. It was so close that we could see the white under its jaw and on its belly.

"Oh, no!" I cried. "It's coming right for us."

But the whale fell backward and hit the water with a great splash. It was amazing, but a little scary.

"Ay, mateys!" the captain cried. "We're in luck today. These are definitely fin whales!"

Fast Fins
by Carlos

   The fin whale is also known as the razorback whale because of a thin ridge along its back. A fin whale is the second largest animal in the world. The fin whale can be 80 feet long — longer than a railroad passenger car. It is one of the fastest swimmers of all baleen whales, cutting through the water at speeds up to 30 miles an hour.

CHAPTER 3

"It was awesome the way that whale jumped up," Arnold said.

"That's called breaching," the captain said. "Some experts think that breaching is a way for members of a group of whales to stay in touch with one another. Or they may be trying to stun their prey while they hunt."

"I hope none of those whales feels like breaching again," I said. "It might fall on top of us the next time."

"Whales seem to know how to behave around people and boats," Captain Gil said. "I've never been toppled by a whale in all my years at sea, but you never can be too careful."

Just then, one of the whales poked its head straight up out of the water. It looked right at us! I covered my eyes.

"It's just checking us out," Captain Gil said with a laugh. "When whales look around like that, we call it spy hopping."

"Ms. Frizzle, I don't want to be spied on by a giant whale," I said. "Get us out of here!"

"I can do something about that, Wanda," Ms. Frizzle said. "Everyone to the cabin!"

"Now what?" Captain Gil asked.

"Uh-oh. Looks like this is turning into another Ms. Frizzle field trip," Arnold told him. "She's always doing this to us."

Ms. Frizzle pushed a red button on the boat's instrument panel. In a blink, the walls curved and the cabin grew longer. The boat had turned into a submarine!

"No more scratching the surface, mates," Ms. Frizzle said. "We're going down deep. We will explore the world of whales in our Magic School Sub. Prepare to dive!"

"Hey, Ms. Frizzle, this field trip is all wet!" Carlos joked.

CHAPTER 4

The bus-sub had a long window along the side. We could see hundreds of fish swimming by — right in front of us! The fin whale we had seen on the surface swam off in the other direction. Everything was quiet except for the faint hum of the engine.

Suddenly, the windows of the sub were completely filled up by the most enormous shape I had ever seen. "Whoa, this is not good at all," I said nervously. "Ms. Frizzle, what is that thing?"

"That's no *thing*," answered Captain Gil. "That is a humpback whale."

Happy Humpbacks
by Tim

The humpback whale's nickname is "Winged New Englander" because of its long white flippers. Humpbacks grow to about 45 feet long, and their tongues alone can weigh two tons!

Humpbacks can live to be 50 years old. If you could count the layers of wax in a humpback's ear, you could find out how old it is.

It was so close to the sub that we couldn't see anything else.

"It's as big as the sub!" said Carlos.

"According to my research, they can weigh up to thirty tons," said Dorothy Ann.

"Look at those flippers," said Ralphie. "They're each longer than a car!"

As the sub made a turn around the humpback, we could see the bottom of its tail.

A Whale of a Name
by Ralphie

   The humpback whale gets its name from the way it curves its back when it gets ready to make a deep dive. No other kind of whale arches its back so high. Also, the fatty pad of skin on the whale's back adds to its humpback look.

"See those markings, mateys?" the captain asked. "Every humpback has a different black-and-white pattern. It's like a name tag or a fingerprint — you can tell one individual from another by its tail markings."

"Let's name this one!" Phoebe exclaimed. "The markings look something like a flower to me. I think a good name for this whale would be Dandelion."

The Tail of a Whale
by Phoebe

A whale's tail is made up of a pair of flukes, with a notch in the middle. The whale swims by pushing the flukes up and down in the water and wiggling the rear of its body. It uses its flippers to steer. The dorsal fin on its back helps the whale stay right side up.

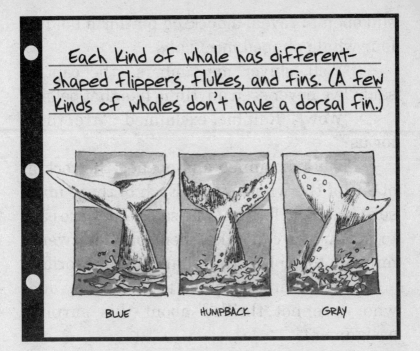

Each kind of whale has different-shaped flippers, flukes, and fins. (A few kinds of whales don't have a dorsal fin.)

BLUE   HUMPBACK   GRAY

"Whales are really interesting," D.A. said. "It would be fun to swim around in the ocean the way they do."

Ms. Frizzle got that twinkle in her eye again. "I have just what you need to dive right in," she said.

She took us to the back of the sub and pushed a yellow button on the wall. A panel slid open to reveal a docking platform holding four whale-shaped mini-subs.

"Well, shiver me timbers," the captain said. "I've never seen anything like that before."

"Wow!" Ralphie exclaimed. "Are these for us?"

The Friz smiled and opened the cockpit of one of the whale subs. "Each of these mini-subs has room for two," she said. "They are easy to steer. You can take them out for twenty minutes to explore the whale's ocean world."

Arnold and I seemed to be the only ones who were not thrilled about this surprise assignment.

"I should have known this wouldn't be a normal field trip," Arnold groaned.

Tim came over to me. "Don't worry, Wanda," he said. "This will be fun. You can be my partner."

"And I will be in constant radio contact with you all," Ms. Frizzle said. "Just call me if you have any questions."

Carlos pulled Arnold down beside him into Whale 1.

Keesha and Ralphie climbed into Whale 2.

D.A. and Phoebe teamed up in Whale 3.

Then Tim and I went aboard Whale 4.

"Don't wander far from the bus-sub," Ms. Frizzle told us, "and keep your eyes open. I expect some swimmingly good reports when you return."

Captain Gil made sure we all had our copies of his handbook. "You might want to check a fact or two during your ocean exploration," he said.

Ms. Frizzle, Captain Gil, and Liz went back into the cabin of the bus-sub. They closed the sliding panel behind them. We were all alone in our mini-subs.

The four mini-subs were lined up facing a spiral opening. Slowly, the spiral turned and water flooded the docking platform. One by one, the little subs slipped silently out into the Atlantic Ocean. The ocean seemed like another world.

CHAPTER 5

Tim and I could see the other whale mini-subs in front of us. Their propellers were making trails of bubbles.

"It's spooky out here alone," I said.

"Relax, Wanda," he said. He was having fun steering the mini-sub. "We're only going to be out here for twenty minutes. Look! There's a school of cod. I wonder what other kinds of fish are around here."

We could hear Ms. Frizzle checking in with the other subs over the radio. Then she contacted us. "Bus-sub to Whale Four, report your status."

Tim picked up the radio mike. "We're

A-OK," he said. "Looks like we're heading into murky waters. What is all this stuff floating by?"

"That's plankton, Tim," Ms. Frizzle's voice answered. "A mixture of tiny plants and animals. Plankton is like a pasture in the sea. It's one of the basic food sources for fish and other sea creatures — like whales."

"Whale Two calling bus-sub." Ralphie's

voice came over the radio. "Something strange is going on. There are lots of bubbles swirling above us. All the fish are swimming away."

"Uh-oh," Keesha cried, "here comes a squid!"

Whoa! Tim and I could see the squid, too. It was swimming fast just above our mini-subs. Its long arms and tentacles looked like they could grab us.

I snatched the radio. "Ms. Frizzle, get us out of here," I yelled.

"Hang in there, Wanda. The ocean may just surprise you," she said mysteriously.

Carlos in Whale 1 came on the radio. "Something is chasing the squid!" he said excitedly. "Something black and white — and very BIG."

"I see it!" Tim called into the mike. "It's . . . I can't believe it! It's a killer whale!"

The orca was closing in on the squid. Its tail churned up the water. Our mini-sub began to rock and roll in the waves.

We heard Ms. Frizzle's voice. "Fasten your seat belts and hold on tight!" I was way ahead of her.

"You are all safe in your subs, but the water might get a little rough," the Friz warned us.

A little rough? It was like being inside a washing machine. Our mini-sub went spinning around and around in the bubbles. Talk about seasick!

Orca the Great

by Tim

The scientific name for the killer whale is orca. These black-and-white whales are often seen in marine parks doing tricks. They are great acrobats.

In the wild, they are fierce hunters. They go after fish, seals, birds, squids, turtles, and sometimes the young of other whales. But they are not known to attack people.

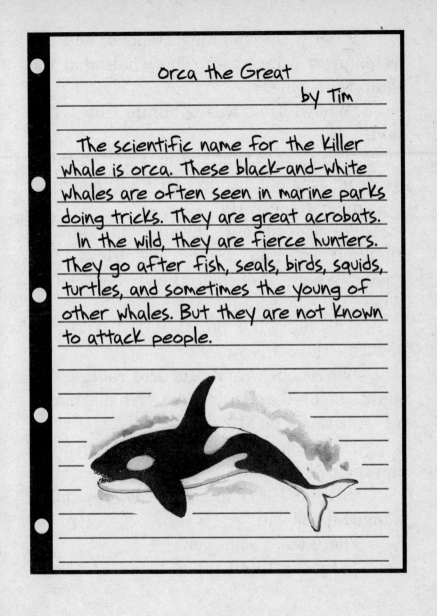

Finally, the spinning stopped, and the water grew calm again. The whale and the squid were gone.

"Whew! That was a bumpy ride," Tim said.

"You can say that again," I said. "I think we're in over our heads!" I'd had enough of this underwater world.

We looked out through the sea of plankton swirling around us. "Hey!" Tim cried. "Where are the other whale subs? Where's the bus-sub?"

"Oh, no. What do we do?" I asked. "I don't see them anywhere."

"We're fine. We've got the radio," Tim said as he picked up the mike. "Whale Four to bus-sub. Come in, Ms. Frizzle."

The radio made an awful crackling noise and then went silent.

"SOS! SOS!" Tim called into the mike. "Come in, bus-sub."

There was no answer.

"Why did this happen to *us*?" I asked.

(By now I was really worried.) "Don't tell me we've lost radio contact."

"We've lost radio contact," Tim said.

"I asked you not to tell me that," I mumbled. "What do we do now?"

"Well, we don't know how far we are from the bus-sub and other whale subs — or even what direction to steer." Tim was thinking out loud. "I guess it's best to stay here. I'm sure Ms. Frizzle will find us before too long." But now even Tim was looking worried.

We stared out the window. Where was Ms. Frizzle? And where were the other whale subs? Were they lost, too?

CHAPTER 6

Meanwhile, in the bus-sub, Captain Gil and Liz were frantically flipping switches on the instrument panel, trying to locate the whale subs.

"Bus-sub to whale subs. Come in, all whale subs," Ms. Frizzle said over and over into the radio.

There was no answer.

"Blasted barnacles!" moaned Captain Gil. "I hope that nothing bad has happened to the little mateys."

"Their radios aren't working," Ms. Frizzle told him, "but I can see four blips on the sonar screen. They're all close except one.

It looks like Whale Four was pulled farther away than the others. I'm sure they'll be all right. But let's get going. As my second cousin A. O'Shun always says, 'The early orca catches the squid.'"

She spoke into the radio again. "Calling all mini-subs. I can see you all on the sonar screen. If you can hear me, stay where you are. Enjoy the scenery. I'm coming to pick you up."

In Whale 1, Carlos and Arnold were staring out the window of their sub. "I knew I should have stayed home today," Arnold said. "Now I'll never get home in time to water my rock collection."

"Don't worry, Arnold," Carlos told him. "I'm sure the Friz will rescue us soon. And look who's there!"

"I don't believe it!" Arnold said. "That whale that just swam by — it was Dandelion!"

"Right," Carlos said. "I saw the tail markings, too. That's definitely the same humpback we saw before."

"Oh, no! It's opening its mouth," Arnold said. "It's huge."

"It looks like a soup bowl," Carlos said, "but big enough to hold a car!"

Open Wide
                              by Carlos

A humpback can open its mouth really wide because it has grooves on its throat that expand like an accordion. It can hold many tons of water in its mouth at one time.

As Dandelion came nearer to the sub, it opened its mouth even wider. "We're going to be lunch. We're going to be lunch," Arnold moaned.

Just then, Arnold and Carlos watched as Dandelion swam past them into a mass of tiny fish and plankton.

When Dandelion's "bowl" was filled, the whale closed its mouth. Then water came rushing out the sides, nearly sending the mini-sub into another wild spin.

Toothless Eaters
by Arnold

Whales that are not toothed whales are baleen whales. Baleen whales don't have teeth. Instead, they have hundreds of long strips of baleen (also called plates) growing down from the upper jaw. Baleen is like a built-in strainer. Water, plankton, and tiny fish called krill go in the whale's mouth. The whale pushes the water out, and the fish and krill are trapped inside.

Each whale "bite" can contain a million or more tiny fish!

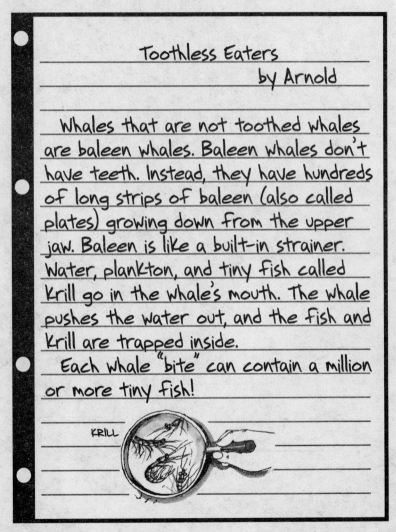

KRILL

"It's a good thing we weren't any closer," said Arnold. "We were almost part of Dandelion's dinner."

Dandelion swam away just as the bus-sub pulled up alongside Whale 1. Ms. Frizzle opened the door to the docking platform and Carlos steered the mini-sub inside.

"Ahoy, mateys!" cried Captain Gil as Arnold and Carlos came into the cabin.

"You wouldn't believe how much a humpback can eat, Captain Gil," said Arnold.

"Humpbacks eat a lot when they're up here in their feeding grounds," the captain explained. "They store up food for the winter, when they make a long journey south. They may not get to eat again for months."

Blubbering Blubber
by Arnold

Whales store their food as blubber — a layer of fat under the whale's skin. Blubber keeps the whale's body warm when it's in cold waters, and the whale lives off its blubber when it's migrating.

"Where are the other kids?" asked Carlos.

"Have no fear, Carlos," said the Friz. "We're on our way to Whale Two. Don't you know that you kids are always on my sonar screen? Liz, set the controls. We're off to pick up Keesha and Ralphie."

From Captain Gil's Whale Watcher's Handbook

Every year, humpbacks migrate from the cold polar waters where they feed to warmer tropical waters. There they mate and have babies.

In the spring, the whales swim back north with the young whales. Humpbacks only swim about 3 miles per hour, but they travel 1,000 miles a month when they migrate.

CHAPTER 7

Keesha and Ralphie had drifted close to a giant log.

"What's that giant log doing in the middle of the ocean?" Keesha asked. Suddenly, the "log" turned over. It was now tilted in the water, tail over head.

"That's no log," Keesha said. "It's a huge humpback."

Then a string of loud moans, squeals, and groans started to come from the direction of the whale. The sounds were so loud that the water around the sub started to vibrate.

"Why is that whale yelling at us?"

Ralphie asked, putting his hands over his ears. "I don't think it likes having us around."

"These sounds are spooky, but they're kind of pretty, too," Keesha said. "It's almost like music."

The sounds went on for a few minutes, then stopped, then started again. "It's repeating the song!" Keesha exclaimed.

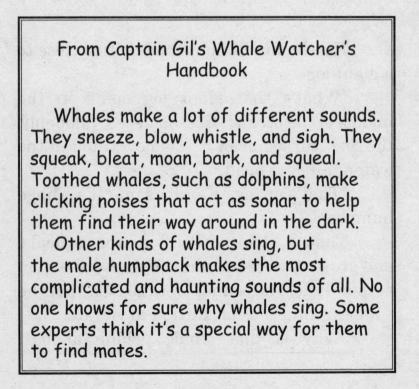

From Captain Gil's Whale Watcher's Handbook

Whales make a lot of different sounds. They sneeze, blow, whistle, and sigh. They squeak, bleat, moan, bark, and squeal. Toothed whales, such as dolphins, make clicking noises that act as sonar to help them find their way around in the dark.

Other kinds of whales sing, but the male humpback makes the most complicated and haunting sounds of all. No one knows for sure why whales sing. Some experts think it's a special way for them to find mates.

"OK, Keesha, try not to flipper-out," Ralphie joked. Just then, Ms. Frizzle arrived in the bus-sub. Keesha and Ralphie joined the others in the cabin.

"The humpback's song is enchanting," Ms. Frizzle said after pausing to take in the sounds, "but we'd best be on our way. There are two more whale subs out there waiting to be rescued!"

While the other whale subs were being rescued, Tim and I were floating along in the middle of a school of tuna.

"I wish I knew where we are," I said, worried.

"Ms. Frizzle's got it under control," Tim said, but he sounded concerned, too.

"Those fish are staring at us," I said. "It feels creepy — like being goldfish in a bowl."

"It's weird that they're looking at us," Tim agreed. "At least we can get out sooner or later. A goldfish has to stay in a bowl all its life."

"We *hope* we'll get out," I said. I was

trying to stay cool, but it was hard just to sit and watch the fish watch us.

We kept trying the radio, but it was completely dead. We were stranded.

In Whale 3, D.A. was checking to see if she had brought along her textbook on radio communication. "It's no use. I still can't get the Friz on the radio," she said.

Even though they were worried, Phoebe

couldn't help having fun watching a humpback mother and her baby. Phoebe and D.A. had named them Mazie and Freckles.

"Freckles is so playful!" Phoebe said. "Look how she keeps tossing that bunch of seaweed with her head."

The seaweed landed on the calf's snout. D.A. and Phoebe laughed.

"Freckles seems to like her seaweed mustache," D.A. said.

Big Babies
by Phoebe

A newborn humpback is about 14 feet long — about as long as a car.

Whale mothers are called cows and their babies are called calves. A whale cow has one calf at a time. A calf drinks 100 pounds of its mother's milk each day! A calf and cow stay together for a year or longer.

While in the warm waters of their breeding grounds, the humpback whale calf feeds on its mother's milk, but the adult whale doesn't eat anything — it lives off its blubber.

Freckles did not swim far from Mazie. Every now and then she would dive under her mother and take a drink of milk.

The two whales swam up to the surface to breathe and then dove back down with

Freckles on Mazie's back. When Mazie swam upward, Freckles slid down her tail. They played this sliding game over and over.

The humpbacks swam away quickly when they heard a noise coming closer.

"It's the bus-sub!" called D.A. "Ms. Frizzle to the rescue! I knew she'd find us."

"I can't wait to tell her about Freckles," said Phoebe.

Captain Gil greeted Phoebe and D.A. with open arms and a big smile. "Welcome aboard, you brave little skippers!" he said.

"We weren't afraid, Captain Gil. Not much, anyhow," D.A. said, patting Liz on the head. D.A. told everyone about watching the calf and its mother. "One thing I don't understand, though. How can a whale not drown if it's born underwater?"

"Good question, matey," said the captain. "Nature thinks of everything! For one thing, the birth takes place near the surface. Also, the baby comes out of its mother's body tail first, not headfirst like a human.

"As soon as the baby is born, its mother

pushes it up to the surface for its first breath. The calf is born knowing not to breathe until its blowhole is out of the water."

"We call that instinct," Ms. Frizzle added. "Instinct is something you know without being taught."

D.A. laughed. "Tim is always saying I have an instinct for science," she said. Then she looked around. "Where are Tim and Wanda anyway?"

"We're on our way to pick them up now. They're right here," Ms. Frizzle said, pointing toward the sonar screen. "That's funny," she said.

"I don't think she means ha-ha funny," said Arnold.

"Whale Four has disappeared from the sonar screen," she told us.

CHAPTER 8

"I'm getting hungry," Tim said. "I wonder if there is anything to eat in the emergency supplies." It was just like Tim to think of food at a time like this. Suddenly, we heard a terrible slapping noise and our whale sub started rocking back and forth.

"Oh, this is bad," I said. "Tim, what *is* that sound?"

Tim was quickly flipping through pages in Captain Gil's handbook, when the book flew out of his hands. The sub was still rocking and everything was falling out of the compartments of the sub.

Tim and I rummaged around the sub,

trying to put things back in place. Nets, life jackets, and flashlights had fallen on top of us.

"Yum, good granola bar," said Tim, popping a big chunk of granola into his mouth.

"Tim, how can you eat at a time like this? We have to *do* something!"

Tim finally found the page he was searching for in Captain Gil's handbook. He looked up with a strange expression on his face.

"The good news is that I think there's a whale out there who is lobtailing. It's slapping its tail against the water over and over again, probably as a way to communicate with its pod. The bad news is, it could go on for a long time. And we'll keep rocking."

A Lot of Peas in a Pod
                    by Wanda

   Many kinds of whales swim in groups
called pods. A pod is like a whale's
extended family and can include 10 to
1,000 whales.

Suddenly, I noticed water pouring into the bottom of the sub. "Tim, we don't have a long time — WATER!"

I grabbed a pail from under my seat. That's when I noticed something I hadn't seen before. There was a button on the control panel with some black letters on it. They read SUR CE.

"Surce?" I said. "What does that mean?"

"Maybe it's some kind of boat word," Tim guessed. "I've never heard of it."

He leaned over to get a closer look. "Wait a minute," he said. "There's space between the R and the C. . . . Hey! The black paint on a couple of the letters got rubbed off. I can just make out the shape of the letters — F and A."

"S-U-R-F-A-C-E," I spelled out.

"Surface?" Tim said. We looked at each other.

"This is a mini-submarine," I said. "Submarines can go up to the *surface* of the water. . . . If we push this button . . ."

"We'll go up!" we both said together.

"Do you want to try it?" Tim asked me.

I wasn't sure it was a good idea. On the other hand — the water was up past our

ankles. And it was getting higher. What if Ms. Frizzle couldn't find us quickly enough? We had to do something fast.

"OK," I said. "Do it."

I held my breath as Tim pushed the button. The whale sub rose slowly. The water got clearer and brighter as we moved closer to the surface.

Then we were there! The ocean water sparkled in the sunlight. We blinked to get used to the brightness.

"Even if Ms. Frizzle can't find us for some reason, maybe a boat or a plane will come by. We'll be OK, Wanda," Tim said.

We looked out over the ocean with our binoculars.

"I see something, Tim!" I called. "Some dark bumps in the water — maybe islands."

"Not unless islands move," Tim said. "Those bumps seem to be floating toward us."

In the next instant, the bumps exploded into the air.

"Whales!" we cried.

Five or six whales were breaching. One

by one, they leaped up and came splashing down. We could see that they had black, tubby bodies with large paddle-shaped flippers, and no dorsal fin. They all had patches of thickened skin on their heads.

Tim checked Captain Gil's handbook. "Those are right whales!" Tim exclaimed. "They're the rarest of all the great whales."

Right On for the Right Whale
by Tim

The right whale can be as long as 50 feet and almost half its weight is blubber. They swim in large pods, feeding and communicating with one another.

Right whales are the most endangered of the great whales.

"What makes them so rare?" I asked.

"The handbook says that whale hunters in olden times killed so many that right whales were nearly wiped out of existence. Whale experts think there are fewer than 500 living in the northern Atlantic. And we're looking at some right now. Wait until we tell Captain Gil about this!"

From Captain Gil's Whale Watcher's Handbook

Humans have hunted the great whales for hundreds of years for their blubber and baleen. Blubber is used for meat and can be boiled to make oil.

The first whale hunters — the Inuit of Alaska — used baleen to make many things including their sleds, spears, and tools. In later times, people found hundreds of other uses for baleen.

The right whale got its name from whalers — this was "the right whale" for them to hunt.

The whales stopped breaching. Most of them disappeared underwater.

"Look!" Tim called. "One of the whales is turning around."

"Oh, no. It's coming right at us!" I said. The huge head was scary. I could hardly watch. "This could be the wrong whale for me," I whispered. "What if it crashes into us?"

I watched as the whale swam once around our sub. Then it lifted one of its big flippers and swam off. I sighed with relief, but the next second it came back. It waved its flipper again.

"It's hard to believe," I said, "but I think that whale wants us to follow it."

"This could be interesting," Tim said. "OK, let's go."

The whale moved slowly but steadily along, never too fast for our sub. Sometimes it held its tail up high, like a sail on a boat.

"That whale is smart," I said. "It's letting the breeze do all the work!"

Watching the right whale sail calmly through the ocean, I forgot to worry about the trouble we were in.

Then, all of a sudden, a line appeared on the horizon.

"Land!" I called. "The whale is leading us home! How cool is that? He's really the *right* whale after all."

Suddenly, we heard a noise behind us. A sleek speedboat came gliding along. It looked something like our Magic School Bus. A man on the deck and a small green lizard were waving their arms. "Captain Gil! Liz!"

"Ahoy there, mateys!" he called. "We got here as fast as we could. How do you like the new boat?"

Soon Tim and I were on board the speedboat. Ms. Frizzle came out on the deck. She was glad to see that Tim and I were all right.

"We had a hard time finding you two," she said. "But it looks like you were heading the right way, toward land. How did you know which direction to go?"

"After Wanda got us to the surface —" Tim said.

"We had some help from a friend," I finished. "A large one with flippers."

"It wasn't just a fluke." Tim grinned.

At that moment our right whale turned back and swam once around the speedboat. Then it dove, lifting its flukes high in the air as if to wave good-bye.

"Good-bye," I called. "Thanks for the help."

Then the whale was gone and we were on our way home. "This was a wonderful field trip," I told Ms. Frizzle. "I never knew a right whale would make me see how wrong I was about whales."

CHAPTER 9

When we walked into the classroom the next day, we got another Frizzle surprise.

One bulletin board was filled with photos of whales with names such as Scooter, Tiny Tim, Sky Rocket, and Angel. A banner read: HELP THE GIANTS OF THE SEA — SPONSOR A WHALE.

Ms. Frizzle clapped her hands to get our attention. "Attention, class," she said. "I have important news. We are about to get a new classmate."

We looked at one another. "Is it a boy or a girl?" Phoebe asked.

"It could be either," Ms. Frizzle said.

"You get to choose. We're going to help take care of a whale!"

"Excuse me, Ms. Frizzle," I said, "but I don't think a whale will fit in the classroom, or even in the gym."

Ms. Frizzle laughed. "Our whale is going to stay in the ocean, where it belongs," she said. Then she explained what it was all about.

"First we need to raise money to pay the sponsorship fee. I thought we could sell our shell and rock collection that we picked up at the end of the whale watch."

Liz held a seashell close to her heart. "It's okay, Liz. We don't have to sell that one," the Friz said.

"Our sponsorship fee," she continued, "will go to a research organization that studies whales and works to protect them from human-made dangers, such as water pollution and illegal hunting. We get a photo of our whale and news reports about where the whale has been seen and what it's been up to."

"Can we choose one of these whales?" D.A. asked, pointing to the bulletin board.

"That's the idea," Ms. Frizzle said. "These whales have been named by the research scientists. They can tell the whales apart by their coloring, scars, special markings, or the pattern of growths on their bodies — such as the callosities on a right whale's head."

We studied the bulletin board. Which one of these whales would we choose to join our class? Scooter was a male humpback. Tiny Tim was a huge male blue whale. Sky Rocket was a female orca, and Angel was a female right whale. There were others to choose from — humpbacks, fin whales, a couple of white beluga whales that lived in waters off Canada, and all kinds of dolphins.

"I think we should get Scooter," D.A. said. "He could sing to us."

"No, it should be Tiny Tim," Ralphie said. "He's the biggest."

Then I spoke up. "I choose Angel," I said. "After all, it was a right whale that helped Tim and me."

"*Right* on, Wanda!" Tim said. "I choose Angel, too."

"Me too," Carlos said. "It seems like the *right* thing to do."

"You've got that *right*," Phoebe added.

"When you're *right*, you're *right*," D.A. said. "I change my vote."

"Well, it looks like Angel is the *right* whale for us," Ms. Frizzle said. "Everyone, say hello to the newest member of the class."

From the Desk of Ms. Frizzle

Save the Whales

Long ago, whale hunting was a big business in many countries, including the United States. Now people use other materials in place of baleen and blubber.

Only a few countries, mainly Japan and Norway, still have a whaling industry. There, minkes, sperms, and other whales continue to be killed for their meat and oil.

Many people think that whales should not be hunted anymore. There are laws that limit the number of whales that can be killed every year. Some kinds of whales — the blue, gray, right, and humpback — are not allowed to be hunted at all. As long as concerned people work to protect them, there will always be wondrous whales in the oceans of the earth.

Whales of the World
by the kids in Ms. Frizzle's class

On this adventure, we found out a lot about fin, humpback, killer, and right whales. There are many other kinds of whales. Here are a few of them. (Look at the map on page 5 to see where they live.)

Blue whale

The largest animal in the world, this baleen whale can be 90 feet long and weigh as much as 32 elephants. Its heart is the size of a VW Beetle car and its eyes are the size of grapefruits.

Blue whales are actually bluish-gray.

Bowhead whale

A relative of the northern right whale, this giant black-and-white baleen whale has lots of thick blubber. It can be 60 feet long and weigh 100 tons.

The bowhead was a favorite of the early whalers. Thousands and thousands were killed. Now there are only about 3,000 to 5,000 left.

Gray whale

A favorite with whale watchers because they are so curious, these baleen whales often swim right along-side the boat so that people can reach over and touch them.

Gray whales can be 40 to 50 feet long. Males weigh about 15 tons. Females are twice as heavy.

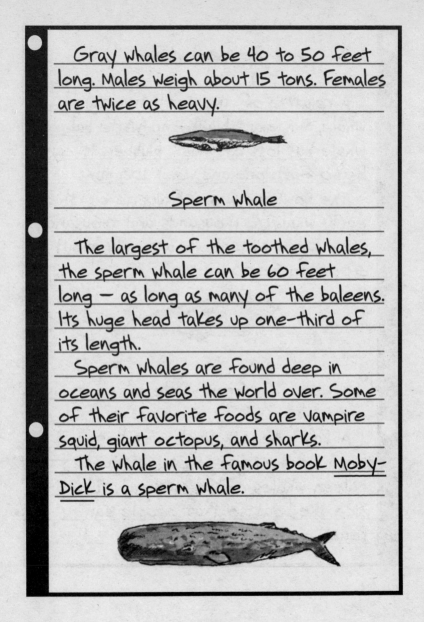

Sperm whale

The largest of the toothed whales, the sperm whale can be 60 feet long — as long as many of the baleens. Its huge head takes up one-third of its length.

Sperm whales are found deep in oceans and seas the world over. Some of their favorite foods are vampire squid, giant octopus, and sharks.

The whale in the famous book Moby-Dick is a sperm whale.

Bottlenose Dolphin

Bottlenose dolphins are a favorite performer in marine parks. Stories have been told about how these friendly, toothed whales have saved people from drowning or taken a swimmer for a ride. But we also know that in the wild they sometimes attack and hurt each other.

Minke whale

Minkes are among the smallest of the baleen whales. A large one is about 30 feet long and weighs 10 tons. They are black or gray with white on their belly and a white "armband" across the flippers.

Beluga Whale

These toothed whales are about 13 feet long and weigh 1 to 1½ tons. Beluga calves are dark gray, but turn white by the age of four or five. Their white color helps belugas blend in with the snow and ice of their Arctic homes.

Belugas are called "sea canaries" because they are always squealing and chirping like birds. They are among the most vocal of all the whales.

Narwhal

Many people say that the legend of the unicorn came from the narwhal. Its horn is really a tooth that cuts through the upper lip and keeps growing until it becomes a tusk 5 to 10 feet long. Some narwhals have two tusks.

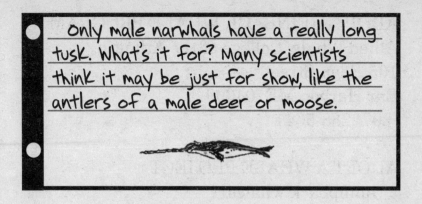

only male narwhals have a really long tusk. What's it for? Many scientists think it may be just for show, like the antlers of a male deer or moose.

Sponsor a Whale

You or your class can sponsor a whale. On the next page are the names of some organizations to contact for information.

If you're thinking about sponsoring a whale, remember to make sure you have an adult make the long-distance call or write to the sponsor program you are interested in to find out more information. Happy whale watching!

ADOPT-A-FINBACK WHALE PROGRAM
Allied Whale, College of the Atlantic
105 Eden Street
Bar Harbor, ME 04609
(207) 288-5644

ADOPT A WHALE PROJECT
  (humpback whales)
Pacific Whale Foundation
Kealia Beach Plaza Suite 21
101 North Kihei Road
Kihei, Maui, HI 96753
(800) 942-5311

ORCA ADOPTION PROGRAM
The Whale Museum
P.O. Box 945
62 First Street
Friday Harbor, WA 98250
(360) 378-4710

RIGHT WHALE ADOPTION PROGRAM
New England Aquarium
Central Wharf
Boston, MA 02110
(617) 973-5253